Fables from the Garden

Fables from the Garden

Leslie Ann Hayashi

Illustrated by

Kathleen Wong Bishop

A KOLOWALU BOOK
University of Hawai'i Press
HONOLULU

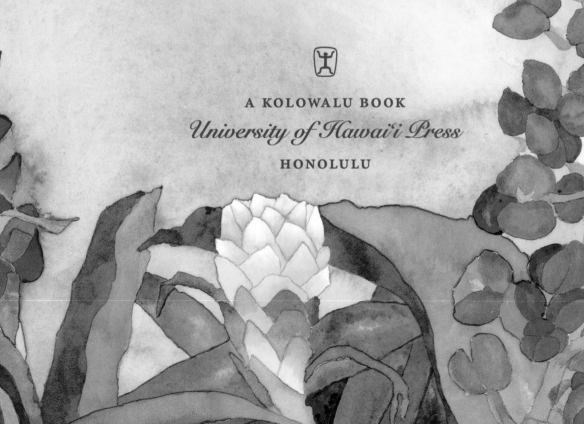

To Alan, for the gift of love; to Kath, for the gift of friendship.—Les

For David, whose love helps me grow.
For Leslie, whose faith makes me paint.—Kathy

© 1998 University of Hawai'i Press

All rights reserved

Printed in Singapore

98 99 00 01 02 03   5 4 3 2 1

Library of Congress Cataloging-in-Publication Data

Hayashi, Leslie Ann.
Fables from the garden / written by Leslie Ann Hayashi ;
illustrated by Kathleen Wong Bishop.
p.   cm.
Summary: A series of brief stories about animals and plants of Hawaii,
each with a moral, such as "Friends respect, appreciate, and even celebrate
each other's differences," and "Excuses are like clouds; they carry no weight."
Includes scientific facts about the featured plants and animals.
ISBN 0-8248-2036-3 (alk. paper)
1. Fables. 2. Children's stories, American. [1. Fables. 2. Short stories.
3. Plants—Fiction. 4. Animals—Fiction. 5. Hawaii—Fiction.]
I. Bishop, Kathleen Wong, ill. II. Title.
PZ8.2.H35Fab 1998
[Fic]—dc21   97-52941
                                                   CIP
                                                    AC

University of Hawai'i Press books are printed on
acid-free paper and meet the guidelines for permanence
and durability of the Council on Library Resources

Contents

The Orchid and the Roses

One day, in a beautiful rose garden, a small potted plant was set near a row of tall rose bushes. Only a foot high, the new plant had just a few broad sturdy leaves instead of the many smaller delicate leaves of the elegant roses. Its thin white roots did not burrow into the ground but climbed all over the sides of the gray cement pot. Unlike the rose bushes, adorned with many colored blossoms, the plant had only two tiny buds near its center.

The stately roses studied the new addition to the garden with great curiosity.

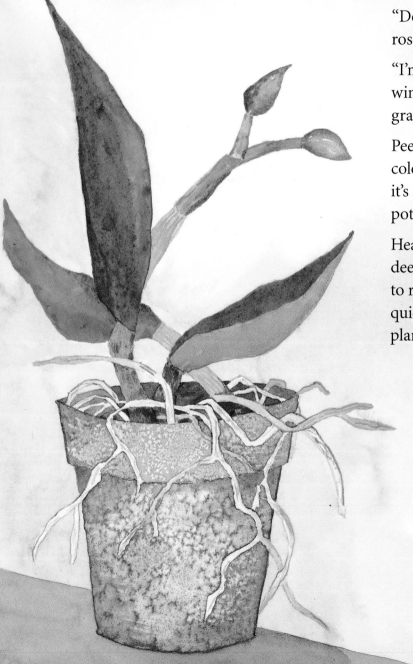

"Do you suppose it's real?" a yellow rose whispered.

"I'm not sure. It doesn't dance with the wind," a pink rose answered, bending gracefully in the breeze.

Peering into the gray pot, a peach-colored rose remarked, "I don't think it's a plant at all. There's no soil in the pot, only rocks."

Hearing their comments, the plant was deeply hurt and couldn't bring herself to respond. Hearing no reply, the roses quickly lost interest in the mystery plant.

One day, the plant's purple buds, which had grown almost as large as the plant itself, opened. The roses stared in awe at the light purple flowers hanging side by side like two large stars. In each of their dark purple centers was a splash of yellow like the warm smile of an early morning sun.

"What beautiful flowers!" exclaimed the red rose. "Do they have a scent?"

The peach rose bent over and sniffed. "Yes, but faint like yesterday's rain—nothing like our fragrant perfume."

"The flowers don't have as many petals as our blossoms and they're not round!" The pink rose sounded confused.

Leaning over, the yellow rose asked, "Excuse me, what kind of plant are you?"

The plant did not answer.

"Perhaps it can't hear," murmured the peach rose.

"Perhaps it can't speak," added the pink rose.

Finally the potted plant could not remain silent any longer.

"I am an orchid," she stated firmly.

"A what?" cried the roses.

"An orchid, o-r-c-h-i-d," the plant repeated.

"An orchid? You're so different from us. You live in a pot and your roots don't spread through the ground. Your leaves and blossoms are—"

"Excuse me, but I've heard all of your comments before. Orchids and roses are different. That's why I seem strange to you even though I'm not at all strange."

8

The roses fell silent for a moment.

"Oh, we're terribly sorry. We didn't mean to hurt your feelings," the red rose apologized.

"We simply forgot our manners. Please, please, forgive us," the pink rose added quickly.

"Let's enjoy the lovely sunshine and the gentle breeze together," the yellow rose suggested eagerly.

"Yes, let's be friends!" the roses chorused together.

The orchid looked at their eager faces. The roses had not meant to be mean; they had simply been curious. Although roses and orchids look different, together they made the garden a very special place. Slowly the orchid smiled, knowing they would be wonderful friends for a very long time.

Friends respect, appreciate,
and even celebrate
each other's differences.

The Gorgeous Chameleon

Once there was a young chameleon who lived in a beautiful garden. This chameleon was quite vain. Every day he strutted about, showing off his bright green colors for everyone to see. He was quite sure he was the most handsome of all the creatures in the garden.

"I'm the best looking," the vain chameleon announced to a large toad burrowed near the gardenias.

"Perhaps you are—in **this** garden. What about the rest of the world? I bet there are better-looking creatures out there," retorted the toad, motioning to the world beyond the fence.

The chameleon had never thought about the rest of the world before. Surely there could be no one better looking than him anywhere!

After the toad hopped away, the chameleon climbed the garden fence. He wanted to see others for himself to make sure he was the most gorgeous of all.

In the next yard he found a small pond filled with brightly colored fish. Climbing out on a bird-of-paradise to take a closer look, the chameleon caught sight of his own reflection.

"Oooh, I **am** so gorgeous," he declared. "No one else is better looking!"

Busy admiring his reflection, the chameleon did not notice a hawk perched quietly above in a large koa tree. *That chameleon could be my lunch,* thought the hawk. Waiting patiently, she watched as the chameleon continued to gaze at his reflection.

Suddenly the hawk swooped down, her talons outstretched! Seeing the hawk's image looming in the water, the chameleon quickly scuttled beneath a nearby ledge. He felt a great *swoosh* from the hawk's wings as they brushed against the rock!

The chameleon's heart pounded and his body trembled. "That was very close," he thought to himself, afraid to move. "I think I'll stay here for the rest of the day," he added, vowing over and over again never to boast about his looks.

Vanity can be harmful to your health.

The Dragonfly's Heart

Beneath the shade of several large monkeypod trees, the mother dragonfly dipped her heavy abdomen into the quiet stream. Gently she laid her eggs, one by one, into the calm water near some floating branches. Knowing she would not live to see her eggs hatch, she could only hope her children would be safe.

However, that night a heavy rain fell, washing branches and eggs downstream. Over rocks and small rapids, they were swept further and further away by the raging waters.

12

In the morning when the flood waters had subsided, several branches drifted near one side of the stream. Next to the bank, the mother dragonfly's eggs came to rest.

All except one. During the storm one egg had been separated from the cluster. That egg continued to be carried further down the stream until finally it nestled among several leaves drifting slowly into a small pond.

In the shallow water the egg began to develop. Inside, cells were dividing, growing into a long body with six legs. One day the protective casing split open. With its gills and thin legs, the brown nymph emerged to explore her underwater world. She found other small creatures— tadpoles and fishes—but no one quite like her.

In the months that followed, the nymph watched in fascination as tadpoles slowly lost their tails and grew feet, then climbed up branches until they were out of the water. Out of the water and into the air! The thought of climbing out of the pond and breathing air filled the nymph with great excitement.

She also observed little fishes grow, find their mates, and swim happily away. Turtles swam with their friends in the pond. Then they too left, returning with their own young. Sighing, the nymph realized she was the only one of her kind. Maybe one day, she would find others like herself . . .

A week later, the nymph met an old turtle who came to swim in the little pond.

"Good morning, Mr. Turtle," the nymph greeted the visitor.

"Good morning, young dragonfly." The old turtle nodded back.

"Excuse me, I think you've mistaken me for someone else," replied the nymph.

"What's that?" the turtle asked. "Don't you know what you are?"

"Oh, yes. I'm a water creature."

"No, look up there." The old turtle pointed to a winged creature hovering above the water. "You're one of those."

Looking up, the nymph saw a beautiful blue-bodied dragonfly. As she watched the wondrous creature skim gracefully over the water, she felt something in her stir.

"Me, a dragonfly?" The thought of being such a marvelous creature filled the nymph with such tremendous excitement that she could hardly breathe. Suddenly, somewhere in her heart, she knew it was true. She was a dragonfly!

Overhearing their conversation, a small fish remarked, "Excuse me, but I don't think that's possible. Dragonflies have slender blue bodies and large wings. Look at her. She's the color of mud, her body is fat, and she has no wings! I don't mean to be rude but look for yourself."

14

"Oh, one day she'll be a dragonfly! Mark my words," the turtle replied.

The fish shook his head in disbelief and swam away.

The old turtle turned to the nymph. "Your heart knows the truth. Listen to it."

More months passed and the nymph shed her skin many times. With each new skin, the nymph remembered the old turtle's words. *I am a dragonfly,* her heart beat over and over. No one paid any attention to her changing body. If they had, they would have noticed wings on her back, growing larger each time she shed her skin.

15

Then one day the urge to be part of the sky and breathe fresh air overwhelmed her. She found a branch and carefully climbed upward out of the water until she found himself surrounded by the smell of sweet strawberry guava. Her little pond looked even smaller from above.

Within hours her outer skin split open for the last time. Struggling, the dragonfly squeezed her new body out of her old skin. At first the breeze could not lift her heavy crumpled wet wings. But within a few hours her wings dried strong and were ready for flight. Her dull fat brown body was gone! She was sleek, her body a beautiful iridescent blue, and her wings shimmered as she spread them in the sunlight.

Flying above her little pond, the dragonfly bid farewell to the old turtle.

"Goodbye, Mr. Turtle. Thank you!"

"You're welcome, young dragonfly. Where are you going?"

"To look for others like me!"

"Then fly far and fast in that direction." The old turtle pointed further up the stream. "Follow your heart."

It was not long before the dragonfly discovered others just like her basking above the quiet waters. As she joined her brothers and sisters, the dragonfly's heart sang with joy!

Listen to your heart to find your true self.

Kathy Bishop

The Fighting Mynahs

One early morning before the dew disappeared, two large mynah birds spied a ripe mango hanging from a tree. Sheltered from the hot sun, nourished by the rain, the fruit was perfect—a shining jewel fit for a king.

The first mynah, an older bird who had survived many storms, moved toward the mango, cawing, "I've lived longer than you. I will eat this perfect fruit!"

Having never lost a fight, the second mynah answered, "I will rule after you're gone so the mango should be mine!"

Puffing out his chest and flapping his wings, the first mynah cried, "You're vain and have much to learn."

"You're old and can learn no more," replied the younger bird, pushing out his chest.

Rising into the air, the mynahs challenged each other again and again, making a huge racket and stirring up dust and small stones. In the midst of their battle, a mother and father sparrow pecked small pieces from the mango to feed their large hungry family. Flying back and forth from the nest to the fruit, the sparrows carried piece after piece into their fledglings' open mouths. Finally the children were full and fast asleep.

After hours of squabbling, both mynahs collapsed, tired and hungry. As they turned to look at their prize mango, much to their surprise, they saw hardly anything was left.

Sharing is better for our stomachs and our souls than fighting.

The Flower That Wanted to Fly

One sunny morning a large monarch butterfly landed gently on a crown flower bush.

"Good morning, dear friend. May I have a drink of your nectar?" asked the butterfly, resting her wings.

"Good morning, my friend; of course you may," replied the flower.

As the butterfly sipped, the crown flower gazed admiringly at her. He remembered when she had been a baby caterpillar crawling along his leaves, growing larger and larger each day. Then one day the caterpillar had fastened herself to a branch. Around and around her body she wound a light, fine thread until she was completely tucked away inside a white cloud.

One early morning, her cocoon split open. She had become a butterfly! Clinging to the crown flower's leaves, the young butterfly looked like nothing more than a wet bundle. Fat like a bumblebee, her wings were damp rags. Then she started contracting her plump body, causing the fluid to course through her wings, making them stiff. Within hours her wings were strong enough to soar on the wind—and she flew away!

It was that moment of flight—of freedom—that filled the crown flower with envy. The butterfly had wings to soar high above the earth, but the flower's roots kept him tied to the ground. The butterfly was free to travel for miles, but the flower would never see beyond his garden. For the first time in his life, the crown flower knew sadness.

"Where did your travels take you this time?" the flower asked the butterfly softly.

"Today I traveled to the sea. So many shades of green and blue! The sun makes the entire ocean sparkle!"

As the butterfly turned to leave, tears flowed quietly from the flower. He watched the butterfly fly up and over the fence like a tiny kite, the sun highlighting her orange and black markings.

Then in that instant, the crown flower realized something. He was the one who had always given the butterfly food and shelter. He was the one who would always protect her from her enemies!

And this time, as the crown flower watched the butterfly on her journey, he too was flying.

There are many ways for each of us to soar.

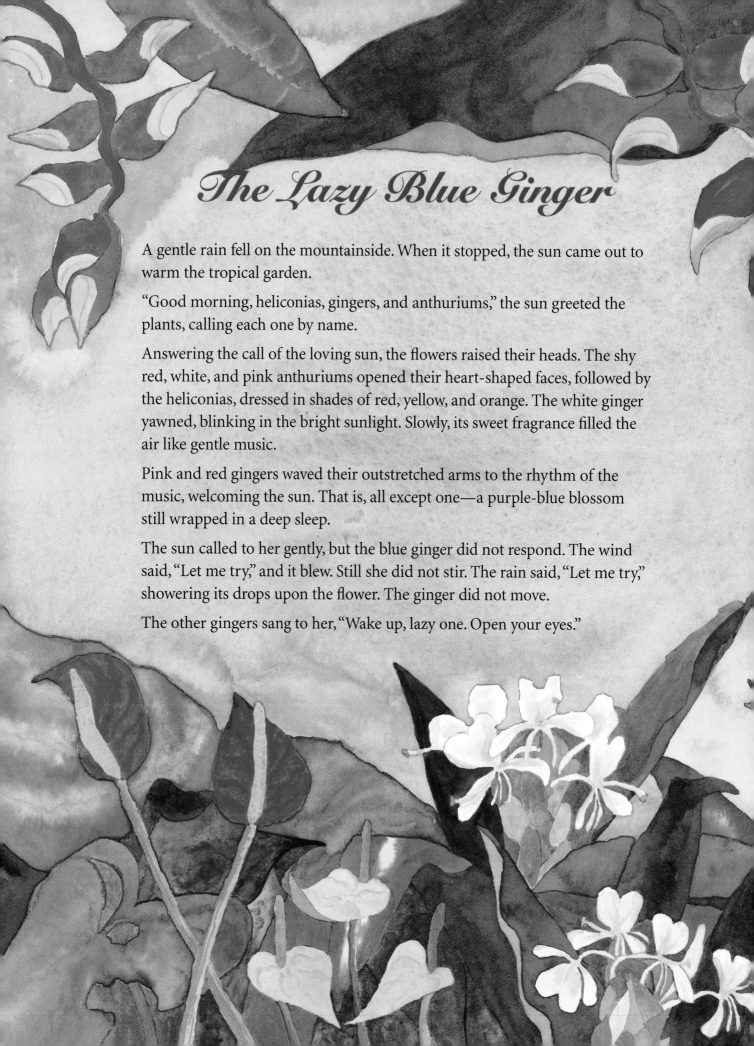

The Lazy Blue Ginger

A gentle rain fell on the mountainside. When it stopped, the sun came out to warm the tropical garden.

"Good morning, heliconias, gingers, and anthuriums," the sun greeted the plants, calling each one by name.

Answering the call of the loving sun, the flowers raised their heads. The shy red, white, and pink anthuriums opened their heart-shaped faces, followed by the heliconias, dressed in shades of red, yellow, and orange. The white ginger yawned, blinking in the bright sunlight. Slowly, its sweet fragrance filled the air like gentle music.

Pink and red gingers waved their outstretched arms to the rhythm of the music, welcoming the sun. That is, all except one—a purple-blue blossom still wrapped in a deep sleep.

The sun called to her gently, but the blue ginger did not respond. The wind said, "Let me try," and it blew. Still she did not stir. The rain said, "Let me try," showering its drops upon the flower. The ginger did not move.

The other gingers sang to her, "Wake up, lazy one. Open your eyes."

"Come play!" cried the heliconias.

"Show us your smile," chanted the anthuriums.

No one could wake the sleeping ginger.

Finally, a pink ginger nudged her, whispering, "Sister, why don't you join us?"

"Oh, the sun makes me drowsy and the ground is so warm. I don't want to get up. Besides, I'm just one flower. The garden is already filled with so many colorful blossoms, I won't be missed," she whispered back.

"We're all part of a great garden. Without you the garden is incomplete."

"Am I needed?" she cried in surprise.

"Join us and see for yourself."

And she did. The ginger opened her vibrant purple-blue blossoms, delighting everyone.

The sun smiled. "At last you are part of the garden's beauty!"

The blue ginger blushed, thinking of the time she had wasted by being lazy. Smiling back at the sun, the blue ginger promised faithfully, "I will **never** sleep late again."

If you are lazy, you may never bloom.

The Excuse Bug

"Mommy, I can't do it." The little Chinese rose beetle dropped the big croton leaf he was carrying.

"Why not?" The mother beetle looked at her son standing next to the fallen leaf, his wings drooping.

"Because I can't. I'm not big enough." Tears were falling down his cheeks and splashing onto the leaf.

"But you're already taller than your brothers and sisters," his mother answered patiently.

"Then I'm not old enough."

"All your friends are much younger than you," his mother answered softly.

"Then I'm not strong enough."

"Only yesterday you lifted many leaves," his mother answered sweetly.

"Then I'm not smart enough," the little beetle pouted.

"But you were the one who discovered that we could keep out the cold winds by using these leaves in our home," his mother answered lovingly.

"I know, but . . ." The young beetle looked about and sighed.

The mother beetle hugged her son.

"Enough excuses, my son. Please don't tell me why you can't do it. Instead tell me that you **can** do it!"

Wiping away his tears, the little Chinese rose beetle picked up the croton leaf.

"I **am** tall, I **am** strong, I **am** smart, I **can** do it," he said to himself over and over as he worked.

Weeks later when the strong storm winds blew, the Chinese rose beetle family was warm and cozy in their home, sheltered by the croton leaves.

Excuses are like clouds;
they carry no weight.

The Bird Who Fell
from the Nest

Inside the mother cardinal's nest lay three speckled eggs. One was much larger than the other two, which worried the red-crested cardinal. Sometimes large eggs never grew into baby birds. Sighing, the mother cardinal knew she could only wait.

She did not have very long to wait, for it was the large egg that hatched first. Pecking a wide hole through the shell, the baby bird let in the light and air. He was completely out of his shell before the others began stirring.

As the days passed, the first baby bird grew bigger and stronger than his brother and sister. Flapping his wings, he wanted to fly!

"No, you must wait until your brother and sister are ready," his father instructed.

"Yes, you must wait. There are many dangers and you need to be strong before leaving the nest," his mother added.

The baby bird did not want to wait. One day when his mother and father were out gathering food, he stepped out of the nest and onto a branch. He spread his wings. A gentle breeze ruffled his feathers. Oh, the air felt so wonderful!

26

Suddenly, a gust of wind toppled the young bird, sending him falling, falling, falling to the ground. He looked up. High above him, his brother and sister peered over the nest. Their squeaky cries quickly brought their mother and father back.

"Why didn't you wait?" his mother wailed.

The young bird chirped back, "Save me, mother." He had wanted to fly. He never thought he'd be stuck on the ground and in danger! He wondered if he would ever see his nest again.

"Stay hidden in the tall grass," his father warned. His parents could not lift him back into the nest. The most they could do was guard him until he was ready to fly. **If** he could survive that long.

Suddenly his mother cried out loudly, spying a large black-and-white cat entering the garden. He walked directly toward the little bird.

"Remain very still! Cats pounce only if you move. Do not run, even if the cat gets near you. I'll lead him away," his father called out.

Whistling, the father cardinal flew to the other end of the garden. Landing on the ground, he hoped to entice the cat toward him. But the cat was not at all interested in the bird. He was busy looking for a warm sunny spot to nap.

Soon the cat found the perfect spot—just five feet away from the baby bird! The cat lifted his right paw, licked it, and washed his right ear. Then he lifted his left paw, licked it, and washed his left ear. Yawning, he lay down, curling up and closing his eyes.

By now both parents were frantic. How could they get the cat to leave? Chirping and calling, they circled above the cat. He twitched his ears. The father and mother circled again, this time lower, squawking louder. The cat opened one eye. He was not hungry. He just wanted to nap undisturbed. Finally he roused himself, slipping out of the garden in search of quiet.

Later that afternoon, following his parents' instructions carefully, the young bird hopped onto a small bush. Each time he jumped higher from branch to branch, he stretched his wings to catch the air. Finally, fluttering then flapping his wings, he felt the wind lift him! Beating his wings faster and steering with his tail feathers, he rose above the nest, hovering for a few seconds before landing safely.

His nest! Never had he felt so grateful to be home! His brother and sister hugged him. His mother and father rested wearily on a nearby branch.

29

Be patient until you are ready to leave the nest.

The Stubborn Cucumber

In a large vegetable garden lived a father and mother Japanese cucumber plant and their three children. The firstborn was a strong plant, always thirsty and always drinking. The second was an adventurous plant, sending his roots out deeper and his vines out farther than anyone else.

The third plant was very stubborn. From the beginning, she refused to dig her roots deeply into the ground. And she refused to grow very many leaves. Day after day she sat still while her family grew taller and taller. Soon their vines were covered with beautiful yellow flowers from which long green cucumbers would grow.

"Sister, please come grow with us," her first brother called out.

"Yes, sister, it's wonderful to have flowers blooming and cucumbers growing," her second brother announced excitedly.

"Little one, it's important to reach out and be part of both the earth and the sky," her parents added wisely.

The little cucumber shook her head. Nothing her family could say would make her grow. Her mind was made up!

One day the farmer and his young son came to inspect their garden.

"We'll have a fine crop of Japanese cucumbers this summer," the farmer observed, pointing out the young cucumbers to his son.

"Daddy, look! There's one plant that's hardly growing."

The farmer stooped over to peer at the little plant.

"You're right. It's not doing well."

"Can we transplant it?"

"It might not survive if we do. Let's check back in a week." Frightened by what she heard, the young cucumber plant turned to her family.

"Mother, Father, and Brothers, please help me!"

Leaning back they let the sun shine on her. They shared their morning dew drops. Day and night the little cucumber worked hard at growing. After all, she had a whole season of growing to do in just one week!

When the farmer and his son returned the next week to inspect the little cucumber plant, they were surprised.

"Look at all those leaves, son!"

"Three, four, five, six yellow buds too, dad!"

"Like a miracle," commented the farmer as they walked away.

And the Japanese cucumber, no longer stubborn, lived to a very ripe old age.

Being stubborn can stunt your growth.

The Little Frog and the Old Bird

Sitting on the edge of a fountain, the little frog sighed contentedly. White clouds drifted across the deep blue sky. A gentle breeze wove itself in and out of the branches of the spreading yellow shower tree. Birds chirped and flowers bloomed under the warm sun. It was another beautiful day, like all the other days she had known.

Suddenly something caught her attention. Beneath a vine with its curtain of pink flowers was a large gray and white albatross.

"Good morning." The frog hopped up to the visitor, curious about him.

"Good morning." The large bird opened one eye wearily. "I need a short rest to complete my journey to the sea. I won't stay long in your garden."

To the sea! thought the frog to herself, breathlessly. She had heard so many wonderful stories about the sea. Perhaps the visitor would be willing to tell her more.

"Oh, by all means. Please make yourself comfortable. Stay as long as you need to. I'll warn you if any cats enter the garden."

As the little frog sat guarding the bird, she marveled at the great white visitor, whose breathing was already steady and soft. The visitor was gigantic compared to the tiny green *mejiro* that flitted in and out of her garden.

While the bird slept, the frog remembered the wondrous tales she had heard of the great ocean. One minute it could be clear and still like glass and then in the next, it could summon waves higher than any tree the frog had ever seen. And the variety of the sea creatures—from the tiniest shrimp to the majestic whale—just the thought filled her with great excitement.

"Are you rested?" the little frog asked when she saw the bird slowly open his eyes.

"Yes, thank you very much, my little friend."

"Can you please tell me stories about the ocean?" The little frog could hardly contain her anticipation as she rocked from side to side.

"Haven't you seen the ocean?"

"No, never. I've lived all my life by this fountain." The old bird could not help but notice the little frog was sad as she spoke.

"I'm too old to carry you on my back. But I'll gladly show you the way so that you may see the ocean for yourself. Only it will be a long journey for you."

"Oh, thank you!" The little frog could hardly believe her luck! It didn't matter how long the journey would take; she was ready!

So the old bird and the frog set off for the sea, with the frog hopping and stopping to rest, and the old bird gliding and circling back.

It was not until early the next morning when they reached the ocean. Still asleep, the sea was covered by a soft white blanket. Then the sun appeared on the horizon, lifting the white clouds on its yellow shoulders. The ocean stretched endlessly until it nestled against the sky. The little frog wondered if the sea and sky were great friends.

The old bird brought the little frog to a tide pool. There in the clear still water were many of the sea's treasures that the little frog had heard about.

A rock crab waved to her. Spotted sea cucumbers moved ever so slowly along the sandy bottom. She watched in delight as a black sea urchin moved its spines in every direction.

All day long the little frog admired the ocean as it sparkled more radiantly than she had ever imagined. At that moment she was both the happiest and the luckiest frog on earth!

When we journey
beyond our own gardens
we realize the splendor
of the world.

Plants

Blue Ginger

Wands of purple-blue flowers wave majestically at the top of its tall stalks. Preferring damp, cool, shady areas, these plants are often seen in valleys that shelter them from direct sun and wind. This Brazilian ornamental is not a member of the ginger family but is related to the wandering Jew, a common houseplant, and to *honohono* grass.

Japanese Cucumber

Japanese cucumbers are grown year-round in Hawai'i. Bees and other insects pollinate the yellow cucumber flowers, which remain attached to the fruit until removed at packing time. By wiping with a damp cloth, the small spines and the whitish, powdery material on the skin, called "bloom," are removed, leaving the glossy, green fruit found in the supermarket. Growing to a length of seven to ten inches, the Japanese cucumber is longer and more crisp than other cucumber varieties.

Orchid

Hobbyists enjoy creating new hybrids, and there are now millions of species of orchids growing in all sizes, shapes, and colors. Sometimes a single flower grows at the end of the stem while other kinds of orchids have clusters of blossoms. Needing air to grow, orchid roots sprawl over rocks, fir bark, moss, and trees. The *Cattleya labiata* or autumn cattleya was introduced to Hawai'i from Brazil.

Birds

Albatross

The Laysan albatross, or *mōlī*, has a natural pair of sunglasses. Black patches around its eyes help reduce the sun's glare on the water. With a wingspan exceeding the height of most human beings, the Laysan albatross is extremely graceful over water, feeding on squid and the eggs of flying fish. On land, however, the Laysan albatross's movements are clumsy, thus earning it the nickname "gooney bird."

Cardinal

The young cardinal has a brown head and black bill. As it grows older, its coloring changes. Its head becomes an easily recognizable bright red color, while its bill turns silver with the rest of its body becoming white and gray. Both sexes are identical in coloring, unlike other species in which the male is more colorful than the female. Red-crested cardinals, or Brazilian cardinals, arrived in Hawai'i from South America in the 1930s.

Hawaiian Hawk

Seen soaring above grasslands and canefields, the Hawaiian hawk, also known as *'io*, symbolized royalty in ancient Hawaiian legends. The state's only native hawk is found on the island of Hawai'i. Its diet consists primarily of rodents, insects, and small birds.

Mynah

The mynah is actually no more quarrelsome than other birds. However, when two mynahs engage in a fight, the others form a ring to watch. Often seen and heard gathering noisily in roosting trees, mynahs are among the most commonly found birds in Hawai'i, along with sparrows and cardinals.

Insects

Chinese Rose Beetle

With their voracious appetites, Chinese rose beetles are considered one of the top ten backyard pests in the state. The grubs or babies feed underground on roots and organic matter. The adults are reddish light brown in color, about half an inch long, and have very short antennae. Adult beetles are seldom seen since they feed at night. During the day they hide in the ground.

Dragonfly

Some people eat while they're on the run; dragonflies eat while they're flying. Two pairs of wings, each with intricate vein patterns, make dragonflies strong and graceful fliers, hovering and gliding over water and open fields while catching insects. Like butterflies, dragonflies develop through several stages. In Hawai'i the nymph or naiad takes about five months before it climbs out of the water to become a dragonfly. There are eight known species of dragonflies in Hawai'i. One of them, the *pinao*, which is found only here, is the largest dragonfly in the United States.

Monarch Butterfly

The monarch butterfly belongs to a family called the "milkweed butterflies," named for the plants they feed on. Introduced to Hawai'i in the 1840s, monarch larvae feed on the leaves of the crown flower, a type of milkweed. The monarch butterfly transforms itself from a caterpillar to a butterfly while encased in a cocoon. The best time to find monarch cocoons is December through February. In about ten days the adult butterfly will emerge. Sometimes you might see a monarch butterfly drink from a flower. The butterfly has a long straw or proboscis, which uncoils to reach the nectar in the flower's center.

Reptiles and Amphibians

Chameleon

The green anole lizard is actually a member of the iguana family, although it is often referred to as the "American chameleon."

In Hawai'i these lizards can be seen climbing along fence tops or stems and branches in search of insects and spiders. When protecting their territory, male lizards extend their pink dewlaps or throat fans while moving their heads up and down.

Like true chameleons, the green anole lizard changes colors in response to varying temperatures and humidity levels. Watch for it to change from bright green to brown or gray!

Dart-poison Frog

In 1932 over two hundred green-and-black frogs were released into the upper Mānoa Valley. These frogs, often referred to as "dart-poison frogs" or "poison-arrow frogs," were collected from islands off the coast of Panama and were introduced to help control the mosquito population. Often seen during or after rain showers and on cloudy days, these strikingly colored frogs are only about the size of a quarter.

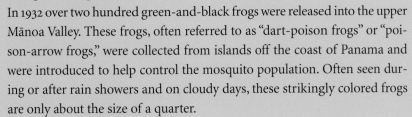

Over 160 different species of dart-poison frogs exist in the world. The skin secretions of some species can paralyze birds and animals, hence giving rise to this frog's name. While the dart-poison frogs in Hawai'i are **not** poisonous, hands should be washed if the frogs are touched. It is better to observe these frogs in their natural habitat than to try to acquire them as pets, since they require very special handling or they will die.

Wattle-necked Softshell Turtle

Living primarily in freshwater streams, ponds, and canals on the islands of Kaua'i and O'ahu, this turtle is rarely seen as it spends most of its life in the water. An agile swimmer, this turtle can remain submerged for over an hour. Using its keen sense of vision and hearing, the turtle feeds on small fish and other aquatic life. The mature female turtle is larger than the male, reaching sixteen inches in length. Both have leathery layers of skin rather than the hard shells of tortoises or marine turtles.

The wattle-necked softshell turtle and the Chinese softshell turtle were brought to Hawai'i by Chinese immigrants in the mid to late 1800s as a food source.

About the Author

Photograph by Jennifer Crites

A graduate of Leilehua High School, Leslie Ann Hayashi received her Bachelor of Arts with distinction from Stanford University and her Juris Doctor degree from Georgetown University Law Center. She serves as a district court judge in Honolulu, where she resides with her husband Alan Van Etten and two young active sons, Justin and Taylor.

Her "Thoughts for a Dead Japanese Fisherman" was the 1995 Grand Prize Winner in the *Honolulu Magazine* / Borders Books and Music fiction contest.

About the Illustrator

Photograph by Wendy Imbornoni

Kathleen Wong Bishop is a graduate of Roosevelt High School and Stanford University. She now resides in Phoenix, Arizona, with her husband David and her three children, Lisa, Daniel, and Rachel.

Ms. Bishop has been a city planner, a community activist, and an educator and is excited to launch her new career as an artist. She has taught Sunday School for many years and is currently the Christian Education Coordinator at Shepherd of the Hills Church. She enjoys helping people explore their spirituality through creative activities.

Growing up in Wahiawā, Leslie's dream was to write and illustrate books with Kathleen, her child-hood friend. *Fables from the Garden* is their debut book and a true gift of friendship.